Secret of the Old Museum

Secret of
the Old Museum

BY ROY WANDELMAIER

Illustrated by Dick Smolinski

TROLL ASSOCIATES

Library of Congress Cataloging in Publication Data

Wandelmaier, Roy.
    Secret of the old museum.

    Summary: The reader's decisions control a series
of adventures inside a museum, including time travel
to ancient Egypt and an encounter with aliens from
the Alpha Centauri system.
        1. Children's stories, American.   2. Plot-your-own
stories.   [1. Museums—Fiction.   2. Space and time—
Fiction.   3. Science fiction.   4. Plot-your-own
stories]   I. Smolinski, Dick, ill.   II. Title.
PZ7.W179Se   1985   [Fic]   85-2533
ISBN 0-8167-0531-3 (lib. bdg.)
ISBN 0-8167-0532-1 (pbk.)

We Hope You Enjoy
This Adventure Story

Just remember to read it differently than you would most other books. Start on page 1 and keep reading till you come to a choice. After that the story is up to you. Your decisions will take you from page to page.

Think carefully before you decide. Some choices will lead you to exciting, heroic, and happy endings. But watch out! Other choices can quickly lead to disaster.

Now you are ready to begin. The best of luck in your adventure!

Secret of the Old Museum

It is Sunday afternoon, and you have reached the end of your rope. Your term paper is due first thing tomorrow morning. If you ever hope to pass with the rest of your friends, you're really going to have to push yourself.

Your assignment was to visit the Cragmore Museum of Natural History (which is only five blocks from your home), and do a report on any of their special exhibits.

Unfortunately, your classmates have already taken the best topics. All that is left for you to choose from is:

LIFE IN ANCIENT EGYPT, or
GEMS AND MINERALS OF THE WORLD

You are standing in the museum lobby with notebook and pencil in hand. It is a beautiful sunny afternoon, and everyone you know is outside enjoying the warm weather. Hardly anyone is in the museum today. You wish you weren't either. But that important paper is due first thing tomorrow morning. Finally you must decide.

If you want to go to the Hall of Ancient Egypt, turn to page 3.

If you want to go to the Hall of Gems and Minerals, turn to page 4.

from page 1

You enter the Hall of Ancient Egypt. There are only a few other visitors today—a group of seven men and women, all dressed in long, white, flowing robes. They are looking at a reconstructed temple.

What interests *you* the most is a new exhibit being set up in a nearby room. Workers are unpacking cases which have just arrived from an archaeological dig. Suddenly a crate crashes to the ground, and the contents spill all over the floor. As the workers scramble to retrieve the artifacts, a small bottle rolls under the partition and rests against your shoe. You pick up the bottle.

The bottle is very old, but it still seems to be full of liquid. It is covered with hieroglyphics, the picture writing of the ancient Egyptians.

The workers are so busy trying to clean up, they don't notice you have the bottle. But the seven men and women in white robes have moved closer to you while you weren't looking.

Did they see you pick up the bottle? Something tells you to hide it in your pocket. You leave the room, but the seven people do not seem to notice you. You walk quickly down a hallway and enter the planetarium to have another look at your find, this time in private.

Turn to page 41.

4

You enter the Hall of Gems and Minerals and get ready to take notes. You've already done some research in the school library, so this shouldn't take long. However, the first thing you notice in this hall are two pairs of small footprints. They look as if they were made with chalk dust. Each print bears the mark of three toes. They lead from a huge meteorite exhibit to behind a temporary work partition. Figuring your report can wait for just a minute, you go take a look behind the partition.

There you meet two small aliens, clutching a chunk of the meteorite.

Turn to page 9.

You, Nisko, and Vleet bribe your way into the palace by slipping a rare gem to a guard. The night sky is lit by all three moons of Alpha Andromeda. You walk down a dark corridor, not quite sure of where you are. Suddenly a voice from behind a door whispers, "Psst. Don't go that way."

If you want to follow the voice and go through the door, turn to page 27.

If you want to keep walking down the hall, turn to page 23.

The liquid smells so good that you take just a tiny sip. It tastes wonderful, too, like honey and cinnamon. You take another sip. The planetarium speaker is saying something about the night sky in August, but the voice sounds like it is coming from underwater. You hear a gentle hum. Then all grows dark around you.

The next thing you see is a camel, walking across the desert. You are sitting beneath a palm tree. It is very early in the morning, and the sun is just about to rise. But all around you, men, women, and children are walking to a marketplace. A huge pyramid is under construction nearby.

The words you hear are a foreign language, yet you can somehow understand every word. You pinch yourself, but you are not dreaming. The liquid must have carried you back in time to the land of ancient Egypt!

Suddenly three men with swords and golden arm-bands walk up to you and ask, "Who are you, and why are you wearing such a strange costume? Answer well, or we will send you to the galleys."

Turn to page 14.

You will go to the mountains for help. But how do you get there? You could take the same geology cruiser that brought you to Andromeda. But the cruiser is slow traveling in the planet's atmosphere. It would take a full hour. You could steal a Voxon sprint ship, which would get to the other side of the planet in minutes.

If you want to take the geology cruiser, turn to page 22.

If you want to steal a Voxon sprint ship, turn to page 20.

from page 4

"Sorriest apologies!" one alien whispers to you.

"Won't you please help us?" asks the second.

You feel sorry for them and decide to help them.

"We are Nisko and Vleet, two geologists. Your scientists would call our planet Alpha Andromeda, in the Alpha Centauri system. We did not mean to land on your planet, but our ship ran out of fuel. This rock contains the element we need to power our ship home."

You lead them safely out of the museum through a service entrance. Their ship is parked behind some tall bushes in the back.

"Thank you," says Nisko. "May we show you our planet? We could bring you back by tonight."

As geologists, Nisko and Vleet could teach you plenty about gems and minerals. And visiting another planet is something you've always wanted to do.

Turn to page 10.

10

Agreeing to go, you board the ship and speed to Andromeda at one thousand times the speed of light. On the way, Nisko and Vleet tell you about their beautiful world and its history. You can't wait to get there.

But when you land your ship in the capital, Andromeda Central, the three of you learn about the terrible things that have happened since Nisko and Vleet left seven months ago.

The evil Lord Snag and his horde of Voxon warriors have invaded the planet. Lord Snag has set himself up in the Andromedan palace. All that was once beautiful on Andromeda is being shipped away to Snag's home planet in the Rigel system.

Rebel Andromedans are hiding in the mountains on the other side of the planet. Nisko and Vleet are experts in geology, but that's about all. They need your advice.

If you want to try to slip into Lord Snag's palace, turn to page 5.

If you want to try to find the rebels in the mountains, turn to page 7.

You take the bottle to the head of the museum's archaeology department, Professor Leopold Brown. A large man, Brown must weigh about three hundred pounds.

He is happy to translate the hieroglyphics for you. He can't give you an exact translation, but the bottle seems to have been created by an order of ancient magicians. The bottle says it contains "the elixir of transformation." Professor Brown returns the bottle to you. He does not know what to make of it.

Just then the door of the office bursts open, and the seven men and women in robes enter. "That bottle is our property," says one of them. "Please return it at once, or we shall have to take it."

Each person holds a gold-handled knife. Professor Brown starts to protest. You are standing next to the back door of the office.

If you want to run out the back door, turn to page 13.

If you feel you have to hand over the bottle to the seven people, turn to page 17.

from page 79

You accept their offer, and they give you $5,000. You turn over the bottle to them.

Now that they have it, the leader takes out a knife from his robe and says to you, "Thank you for being so cooperative. Now we will take back the money."

You have no choice. As they leave with the bottle and the money, you wonder who they were and what they wanted with that strange bottle.

THE END

from page 11

Taking everyone by surprise, you dash out the back door of Brown's office. Your quick decision gives you a head start. But you know they will be following you.

You run down a dark hall and come to an intersection. One way leads to the Hall of African Animals. The other leads to the Hall of Dinosaurs.

If you want to run to the Hall of African Animals, turn to page 18.

If you want to run to the Hall of Dinosaurs, turn to page 21.

14

from page 6

Before you can answer, another voice speaks up from behind you. "Officers, this is one of the new pyramid workers from Mesopotamia. Come on you lazy rascal, get back to work."

You turn to see a tall man dressed in simple clothing.

"Are you saying this stranger works for you, Calik?" asks one of the men with swords.

"Yes," says the man. "Now let us get back to work."

The three men go away. You are left alone with the man named Calik.

"You don't really have to work with us," says Calik with a smile. "I just didn't want you sent to work on the galleys.

"But we certainly could use your help. Building a pyramid is hard work, as you must know. But we can give you some proper clothing, food, and a place to sleep at night."

Turn to page 26.

16

"This bottle does not belong to any of us," you say. "I'm going to turn it over to the museum."

"Don't be foolish!" says the leader. "You could have had this money. Now we're going to take the bottle anyway, and you'll get nothing."

They walk toward you. You threaten to throw the bottle against the floor.

"You wouldn't dare!" says the leader. He lunges at you, but not before you do smash the bottle against the floor.

Smoke rises in a small thick cloud from the floor, and drifts over to a huge stuffed gorilla.

The gorilla comes alive! The men and women in white are terrified. They run out of the hall and leave you alone with the beast. Then something even more unexpected happens.

"Thank you," says the gorilla. "I don't know how you did that, but I was pretty tired of standing here for so many years."

Turn to page 69.

You give the bottle to the seven people. They tie you and Professor Brown to chairs, then leave you in the room. You may be here for a long time.

Fortunately, Professor Brown's colleague, Dr. Amanda Karp, walks into the office. "Who were those people?" she asks.

"No time to explain, Dr. Karp," says Brown. "We've got to find them. But where could they have gone?"

You have a good guess. You lead the two professors back to the Hall of Ancient Egypt.

Turn to page 25.

from page 13

The Hall of African Animals is not like you remember it from last year. The lights have been turned off, and there are no people. Has the museum closed?

In the center of the huge room stand five wild elephants, posed as if they were going to charge. In other exhibits all kinds of African animals stand in their natural habitats: snakes, rhinos, lions, gorillas, and crocodiles.

Unfortunately, the Hall of African Animals is a dead end. The only way out is through the door you entered. But the seven men and women in white are now standing there. You are trapped.

Turn to page 79.

from page 7

You want to get to the mountains as quickly as possible, so you steal a sprint ship. Soon you are speeding away. Unfortunately, some angry Voxon pilots are speeding after you in their own sprint ships.

You can try to outrace them. The mountains are only two minutes away. Or you can try to crash-land in the huge forest below.

If you want to try to outrace them, turn to page 32.

If you want to try to crash-land in the forest, turn to page 35.

from page 13

You run to the Hall of Dinosaurs. On the way, you pass an office door with a sign that says:

Dr. Margaret Walker
Professor of Pre-History

Do Not Disturb

If you want to hide in this office, turn to page 70.

If you want to go on to the Hall of Dinosaurs, turn to page 74.

from page 7

You take the slow geology cruiser and hope for the best. You fly low over the forests and lakes of Andromeda. It works. You pass across the other side of the planet undetected by the Voxons. After you land, you are led inside the rebel stronghold. The three of you are introduced to the rebel leader, Alf Gan-Rosh.

"To defeat Lord Snag, we need the Stone of Narvelin," says Gan-Rosh. "But the Stone is guarded by the Mangons."

"What are Mangons?" you ask.

"Monsters with a keen sense of taste and smell," says Gan-Rosh. "They vaporize anyone they don't like. And we have never known them to like anyone. We must act fast. Time is running out for Andromeda."

You, Nisko, and Vleet discuss the problem. Vleet reminds you that they have collected many unusual minerals from different worlds. Perhaps one of them will be useful to you now. You check the ship's computer. There are three elements which may help.

Element 40, Zenium—brings invisibility
Element 50, Meerang—brings the force of lasers
Element 53, Argonix—brings loss of odor

Go to the page with the same number as the element you want to take with you.

Ignoring the voice, you keep walking down the hall. As you turn a corner, Voxon guards capture the three of you and throw you into an abandoned storage room. (There was never a dungeon built in the Andromedan palace.)

Several guards stand outside your door.

"What is going to happen to us?" you whisper.

"If we're lucky," says Vleet, "we may be sent to work in the Mines of Pluto for the rest of our lives."

"And if we're not lucky?"

Before Vleet can answer, you hear a small scratching noise somewhere in the room. You freeze. Then the scratching turns into a small tapping noise. Tip. Tap, tap, tap. Tip. Tap, tap, tap.

If you want to search the room and try to find what is making the noise, turn to page 37.

If you want to tell the guards about the noise, turn to page 34.

from page 17

By now the museum has closed. Most lights are turned off. Together you tiptoe behind a partition, and see the seven people use heavy iron tools to crack open a newly arrived mummy case. They pour the liquid from the bottle over the mummy inside. The mummy comes to life!

"Awake, pharaoh!" says the leader. "We, the Seven Priests of Amun-Ra, have brought you back to life. With your help, we will control the world!"

The mummy, however, does not seem to want to help these people. He tries to fight, but he is still too weak after remaining undisturbed for over 3,000 years. The priests easily tie him up with rope.

"We just need to get him back to the desert," says the leader. "That will bring him back to his senses. The helicopter should be here by now, Hassan. Take the others and bring our equipment up to the roof. Then come back and get me and the pharaoh. I will stay here until you return. Now move quickly!"

To stop the Seven Priests of Amun-Ra, you see you must not let them take away the mummy.

If you want to send the professors to fetch the museum guards, turn to page 33.

If you want to think of some way to rescue the mummy yourself right away, turn to page 38.

from page 14

You agree to go with Calik. He gives you some cool white clothing to wear. Now you look like a real pyramid builder.

Just as Calik said, building a pyramid is not easy. You strain and sweat, but you do not give up.

That night, after a refreshing meal, Calik takes you aside. "I didn't think you would be such a hard worker," he says. "We are all glad to have you. Now sleep well. But please remember. Do not leave the camp at night. It is not as safe as in the old days. Please do *not* leave the camp for any reason."

You promise not to. And you fall asleep under the stars, next to the great pyramid. Calik sleeps under some trees.

In the middle of the night, something wakes you. You listen, but hear nothing except the cool night breeze.

Then you notice Calik is gone.

Turn to page 45.

from page 5

You walk with care into the dim room. The door closes quietly behind you. Now it is completely dark.

"Who's there?" asks Vleet. Nisko bangs into some metal objects, which clatter to the floor. "We must be in a kitchen," he reasons. "This room is full of pots and pans."

"Shh!" says a strange voice. "Stop that racket. Do you want Lord Snag himself to find us?" A small light comes on, and you see a short figure behind a counter. He introduces himself as Milo Vern, former chef to the Andromedan Royal Family. "I've been hiding in here since the day Lord Snag took over the palace," he says.

"What has happened to the palace?" asks Vleet. "What is Lord Snag doing?"

"Just what he is doing to the rest of our beautiful planet. He is taking away everything of value—our trees, our minerals, our food—even our water. Soon there will be nothing left."

"Are there no other loyal Andromedans left in the palace?"

"None but me," says Milo. "Only Lord Snag's slaves work here now. I have a plan to stop Snag, but I need your help. Will you help me?" You agree to help.

Turn to page 28.

"Today is Snag's birthday," says Milo, "and I'm baking him a cake."

"A poison cake, I hope," says Vleet.

"No," says Milo. "Snag has his slaves taste his food first. The cake can't be poisonous, but it *will* change Snag forever. And no one will notice until it is too late. The cake will be ready in a minute. All we have to do is take it to the main kitchen and replace the real cake with ours."

"There is only one problem with this plan," says Nisko. "Which of us will take the cake into the kitchen?"

"Of course, I would be glad to," says Milo, "but I really don't feel so well. Won't one of you please take it? It is our only chance to save Andromeda."

You, Nisko, and Vleet draw straws. Unfortunately, you choose the short one.

Proud Milo gives you his cake. "Go down the hall, take the second door on your right. Just replace the old cake with this one. They will look exactly alike. All the cooks are on their break now, so the kitchen will be empty. Then just come back here and hide with us. Here—wear my old chef's hat as a disguise, just in case you meet any of the cooks in the hall. They will think you are one of the slave workers brought here from other worlds. Go now, before the cooks return!"

Go to page 29.

from page 28

"But what does the cake do?" you ask. "What's in the recipe?" Milo urges you to hurry. He says he'll explain as soon as you return.

You take the cake and find the main kitchen. Sure enough, the room is empty. Inside, all the food is ready for Lord Snag's feast. You pick up the old cake—Milo certainly has done a fine job copying it—and throw it down the disposal unit. You put the new cake in its place and run to the door. Just then the cooks and a squad of guards return. They are in a panic.

"Spies have been found in the palace," says the head cook. He looks at you, then says, "Hurry! You carry the cake."

The good news is that no one seems to suspect you are a spy. The bad news is that you now have to deliver Lord Snag's birthday cake in person.

In the throne room, a wild birthday celebration is going on. There is Snag: a giant monster with great green horns and claws. Shoveling food into his mouth, he never seems to get full. You hope Milo's cake works. You are certainly glad you won't have to eat it. Then your heart sinks. You see Nisko, Vleet, and Milo caught in a cage. For their sake you pretend you don't know them. An hour of eating passes, then it is finally time for dessert.

Turn to page 30.

from page 29

"Wait," growls Lord Snag. The room rumbles. "I didn't get to be Emperor of the Universe by trusting people. I don't recognize that slave." He means you. "I would like you to taste this cake yourself!" He roars with laughter, and so do all the slaves, servants, and Voxon guards.

"Of course," says Snag, "you have a choice. You can eat the cake or you can join the others in the cage."

If you agree to eat a piece of cake, turn to page 44.

If you refuse to eat the cake, turn to page 48.

from page 20

You try to outrun the Voxons. Their laser beams shoot past you, but your ship is fast and easy to maneuver. The problem is you have no place to land safely. If you slow down, the Voxons will blast you. All you can do is dash away into space.

You may be able to outrun the Voxons and hide on one of Andromeda's moons. But you will probably not be able to return to Andromeda for a while. You hope it won't be too late.

THE END

from page 25

Professors Brown and Karp sneak away and find a guard in minutes. But that is already too late. When they return, the priests and the mummy are gone. All that remains is the empty mummy case. You wonder what the Seven Priests of Amun-Ra have in store for the world in the days to come.

THE END

34

from page 23

You call to the guard, "There's something crawling around in here. Please put us in another room."

"The only thing crawling around will be you three spies," says the guard, "in the Mines of Pluto."

You do not hear the tapping noise again. The next day you are shipped to the Mines of Pluto.

THE END

from page 20

You don't think you can safely outrun the Voxons, so you crash-land your ship in the thick forest below. It works. The Andromedan trees break your fall, and you come to a bumpy, but safe landing.

To your surprise, the Voxons don't follow you. They turn and fly back to Andromeda Central. Seeing your confusion, Vleet explains, "Even the Voxons have heard the stories about the Great Forest of Andromeda. Everyone says it is the most dangerous of places, but no one knows if the stories are true. No one ever comes here. Even if we survived the crash, the Voxons must think we will not get out of the forest alive."

The forest floor is dark. You can't even see the tops of the trees. Barely any light from the Andromedan sun, Alpha Centauri, finds its way through the thick leaves.

"What kinds of stories?" you ask. But before Vleet can answer, you hear a loud roar.

Turn to page 43.

You follow the tapping sound and finally find its source behind the doors of a low cupboard. An Andromedan is crouched inside.

"Follow me," he says. The three of you crawl inside the cupboard, close the small door behind you, and begin to follow a dark passageway. Soon you come to a small room which looks like an abandoned kitchen.

"My name is Milo Vern," says the Andromedan. "And I have been hiding here since Lord Snag took over. I don't know why you came to the palace, but it is too dangerous for you here.

"If you want to help defeat Snag, go to the mountains, and go quickly. Good-bye for now." He disappears back into the passageway.

"I think going to the mountains is a *wonderful* idea," says Nisko.

"Let's get out of here!" says Vleet.

You lead your two scared geologists safely out of the palace.

Turn to page 7.

from page 25

There is no time to look for guards. You have to create some kind of distraction.

"Professor Brown," you whisper. "Go back to the hallway and make some kind of noise. Get their leader out of this room. Do whatever you have to."

"Leave it to me," says Professor Brown.

Now it's up to you and Professor Karp. You wait fifteen seconds, then twenty seconds. The priests will be back any minute to pick up their leader and the mummy. What happened to Dr. Brown?

Suddenly you hear the noise of a horn. The leader is alert. He goes to see what the noise is. Dr. Karp says, "How clever of Dr. Brown—imagine using the horn of Im-ho-tep."

This is your only chance. You and Karp run up to the mummy case and untie the mummy. The mummy is glad to be free. But now the seven priests return, with Professor Brown as their prisoner.

Turn to page 90.

from page 43

It is dangerous in the forest, so you stay safe inside your ship. Realizing no one is going to come and rescue you, you go out and catch some small animals to eat. You start a fire.

As the days pass, you get better at surviving in the forest. Eventually you befriend the forest people. Now you are safe in the forest, while around and above you Andromedan rebels fight their last losing battle against Lord Snag and his Voxons.

Sadly you realize your safety is only temporary. Sooner or later, the Voxons will turn their attention to the riches of the forest. You wonder how much time you have left.

THE END

from page 22

You choose the element Zenium, which makes you invisible. That helps get you through the forest undetected by wild animals. But it doesn't help you with the Mangons. They smell you from a mile away and come flying out at you.

THE END

A sky show in the planetarium is being projected against the high round ceiling. No one in the audience notices you as you take a seat in the rear, with your back to the wall.

You take out the bottle from your pocket. It seems to be made of clay, and you wonder what kind of liquid is inside. You break open the seal and sniff. It is a strange, delicious smell.

If you want to take a sip of the liquid, turn to page 6.

If you want to take the bottle to the head of the museum's archaeology department, turn to page 11.

from page 35

An animal that looks like a lion with antlers leaps through the trees toward you.

You scramble back into your ship. The animal is smart enough not to attack the metal ship, so it sniffs around and looks for other prey. Then, to your horror, you notice two small alien children who have come out of the forest to see what caused the crash. The antlered lion gets ready to pounce on them.

To save the children, you shoot at the animal with lasers from the ship. The Andromedan lion flees! Soon the children's parents arrive, carrying primitive laser guns of their own. But they do not seem to want to go near your ship. They wave their thanks to you, then take their children and walk away into the gloom of the forest.

If you want to follow after them, turn to page 47.

If you want to stay in the safety of the ship, turn to page 39.

You try to remember Milo's rushed words: "The cake won't be poisoned . . . . No one will be able to tell the difference until it is too late." You hope he was right.

You pick up a piece of cake and take a small bite. It doesn't taste bad, just a bit spicy. What will it do to you? You eat the rest of the piece.

Your stomach begins to feel warm, your head feels light. Then you begin to feel better than you ever have in your life. You even begin to see things more clearly.

"This is the best cake I've ever had," you say.

Snag is furious. He grabs the rest of the cake and swallows it whole. "Hmm," he says. "That *was* good."

Then he looks confused. He trembles. He almost faints. Finally he speaks: "Free the prisoners. Stop the destruction. I have made a terrible mistake!"

There is rejoicing throughout Alpha Andromeda. Milo's recipe worked. It turned absolute evil into absolute good. Nisko and Vleet are especially proud of your courage.

The Andromedans present you with rare gems and a ride home. On the way, Nisko and Vleet help you with your term paper. They promise to come back to visit you on Earth. And they provide you with a special device so you may visit them on Andromeda whenever you like.

THE END

from page 26

You check for the bottle. Since it brought you here, you don't want to lose it. It may be your only way to get home again. The bottle is still safely hidden in your clothing, but where is Calik? In the distance you see a lone figure walking away from the camp. You are almost sure it is Calik.

If you want to follow him, turn to page 56.

If you want to remain in camp as you promised, turn to page 51.

Through the jungle you follow the forest people. They seem to know when to hide from giant animals and when to walk safely.

After several hours, you find yourself walking in the foothills of some mountains. Suddenly, the forest people point to what may be the entrance to a cave. Then they walk back to the forest. You and Nisko and Vleet cautiously go inside the cave.

The room is full of Andromedans. You have found the rebel band! The rebel leader, Alf Gan-Rosh, speaks to you:

"We are most glad to have you here. Our spy in Andromeda Central tells us that Lord Snag is growing quite angry with us. Our attacks against his mining operations are slowing him down. Now he is massing a huge force against us. He does not yet know where this cave is, but it won't take him long."

An explosion rips against the side of the mountain. Evidently Lord Snag has already begun his attack. You can't stay trapped in the cave. You must go outside. But where?

If you want to advise the rebels to go higher into the hills, turn to page 82.

If you want to advise the rebels to go down to the forest, turn to page 88.

from page 30

You refuse to eat a piece of cake intended for Lord Snag. So you are put in the cage with your friends.

Because it is his birthday, Lord Snag has mercy on you. Instead of having you as a midnight snack, he will send you tomorrow to the Mines of Pluto. In one hundred years, you may become eligible for parole.

THE END

from page 69

You decide the gorilla would be happiest in its real home, the jungle. You help sneak the gorilla through the dark halls of the museum into the underground parking garage. You all get into Professor Brown's station wagon.

At the pier you smuggle the gorilla safely aboard the ship. You wave good-bye as they prepare for their journey across the ocean.

THE END

50

from page 22

Meerang gives you great laser firepower. But you find you need more than that.

You never even get close enough to their lair before the Mangons smell you. In the battle, you kill many Mangons. But they are finally too much for you. You, Nisko, and Vleet will always be remembered as brave heroes.

THE END

You fall back into an uneasy sleep. When you awake, Calik is back on his bed as if he had never left. You say nothing to him during the day. But after the sun sets, you take him aside and tell how you saw him leave last night.

Calik merely laughs. "I did not go anywhere," he says. "Am I not the one who told *you* not to leave at night? Are you sure you weren't dreaming?"

You know you did not dream it. Why is Calik not telling the truth?

If you want to wait to see if Calik will leave again tonight, turn to page 63.

If you want to take a new sip of the liquid, turn to page 85.

You take the Argonix, which erases any odor you might have.

It is a hard climb through the forest, but you arrive at the Mangons' cave safely. Because the monsters can't smell you, they don't wake up. Now it will be easy to take the Stone of Narvelin and to free Andromeda.

You become a national hero and are given a safe ride home to Earth. There will always be a special holiday in your honor on the distant world of Alpha Andromeda.

THE END

from page 86

Dr. Walker, if she is still alive, must be somewhere in this cold world. But where?

At the edge of the forest you see a faint wisp of smoke. If it is a fire, perhaps there are other human beings here. Perhaps Dr. Walker is among them. There may even be some warm food.

You begin walking toward the forest. Then you hear a noise behind you. You turn to see a herd of woolly mammoths who have discovered your time machine! They pick up the machine. You shout at them, but it is too late. They dash the machine against the ground. Will you ever be able to get back home?

If you think this is bad, a giant saber-toothed tiger has spotted you—and it looks hungry. You run to the nearest tree, but the tiger is gaining on you. You'll never be able to climb the tree in time. Suddenly two hands grab you from above and haul you up into the tree. The tiger lunges at you, but just misses.

Turn to page 66.

After dark, the gorilla's disguise should fool most people. You buy two subway tokens and wait on the platform for the next train.

Then you notice a disturbance at the other end of the platform. It is the seven men and women in white robes! They are robbing passengers, and no one can stop them.

You run to call the police. When the police arrive, all of the seven people have been captured by the gorilla.

You tell the police about what happened in the museum. They find that the seven people are wanted by the FBI—they are an international gang of criminals.

You and the gorilla are local heroes. The mayor gives you a reward. The gorilla gets a first-class ticket back to Africa.

Best of all, your school principal allows you to go along. You still owe a term paper, but now you can choose a new topic: the wildlife of Africa. It should be an exciting trip.

THE END

from page 45

You follow Calik through the dark streets of the nearby village, careful that he does not see you. Soon you lose sight of him. Did he know you were following him?

You are not sure where you are. One street looks like the next. Suddenly a woman in a white robe stands in your path.

"I have noticed you since your arrival here," she says. "May I have a word with you? I am one of the Servants of Amun-Ra. Several months ago, we lost a small object, a bottle to be precise.

"Please don't ask me how, but I believe that you may know something about it. The information you may have is very important. It could save many lives. I am prepared to offer you gold if you can help me. Are you interested in this offer?"

If you want to say you are interested, turn to page 64.

If you want to say you don't know anything about a bottle, turn to page 60.

from page 85

You take another sip. This time your whole body shudders. You turn into a golden eagle. The empty bottle drops at your feet.

As you fly high above the Nile, you see the unfinished pyramid below. The wide river looks so beautiful in the moonlight. You live the rest of your life as a golden eagle.

THE END

Could the bottle you have be the same one wanted by the Priests of Amun-Ra?

You would like to help Calik, but you don't want to give him your only possible way of getting home. You hope the answer will come to you tomorrow. But all that comes to you as you walk back to camp are the Priests of Amun-Ra. They sneak up on you from behind, take the bottle, and leave you alone in the desert.

Now you rush to find Calik, wondering if it is too late to save civilization.

THE END

from page 56

"I'm sorry," you tell her. "But I don't know anything about such a bottle."

Her eyes flash, but her voice is still warm and soothing. "Are you sure?" she asks.

Suddenly Calik appears, walking down the street toward you. You call his name, and the woman disappears down an alley.

Calik hurries over to you. "Are you all right?" he asks. "What did that woman want? And why did you leave the camp?"

If you want to tell Calik what the woman said, turn to page 65.

If you want to say nothing for now, turn to page 67.

from page 81

You follow the servant around to the back of the palace. He is bringing the pharaoh some fresh dates just picked for the royal breakfast. You offer the servant the ring on your finger. You say you only want to serve the pharaoh his dates. You speak the language so well, and your ring is so shiny, that the servant is delighted to let you do his work today.

You enter the palace. You have never seen any building so splendid. The beautiful columns, plants, pools, and painted walls sparkle. Then you see a man alone by a pool. From his clothing, you know this can only be the pharaoh.

Turn to page 96.

from page 51 / from page 71

You decide that if Calik leaves tonight, you'll follow him.

When the moon is above the pyramid, Calik slips away again. You follow him in secret to a grove of palm trees. You climb one of the trees, to watch and to listen. Other men and women are gathered below.

Calik speaks. "We know the Priests of Amun-Ra are ready. Why are they waiting? I believe they still lack the one thing which will guarantee their victory: the potion of Thebes.

"We don't know who stole the potion from the magicians. But I don't need to tell you that if the potion falls into the hands of the Priests, they will gain control over all the Nile Valley and begin a rule of madness and evil.

"Now time is running out. They will make their move soon, with or without the potion. Tomorrow, we must find the potion before the Priests do."

There are no questions. Everyone leaves the grove except Calik, who remains deep in thought.

If you want to approach Calik and tell him about the bottle you found, turn to page 78.

If you do not want to tell Calik, turn to page 59.

from page 56

"Yes," you say. "I think I am very interested, but first may I see the gold?"

"Of course," she says. She takes out a gold-handled knife. "Now give me the bottle." You have no choice, and that is the last thing you remember.

THE END

"I'll tell you," you say, "but not here. Can we walk back to camp?"

On the way back, you apologize to Calik for leaving the camp. But you also remind him that *he* left camp, too. Calik has to laugh at this. Then you tell him what happened with the woman.

"I am glad I arrived when I did," says Calik. "That woman was no servant. She is a Priest of Amun-Ra. All I can tell you about them is this:

"A magicians' potion was stolen recently from the pharaoh's palace. No one knows exactly what the potion can do, and the magicians are not saying.

"The Priests of Amun-Ra want to get this potion before the pharaoh does, and that would be a dark day for all of us. But let us not speak of them in the street anymore. Please go back to camp as quickly as possible." With that Calik walks away.

If you want to go after Calik and tell him about the bottle you have, turn to page 78.

If you do not want to tell Calik, turn to page 59.

If you want to go find a private place to take a drink from the bottle, turn to page 85.

66

You come face to face with a prehistoric man and woman. Together they carry you higher and higher into the tree. The tiger will not follow you up there. You are safe. The man and woman grunt and poke you in the arm. You poke them back, and they smile. They seem to like you.

The tiger soon goes away, and the two people climb down to the ground. They begin to walk away. From your tree-top perch, you see something shiny at the top of a nearby hill. The man and woman are walking in the other direction, toward the smoke in the forest. Soon they disappear behind the trees.

If you want to follow the man and woman, turn to page 99.

If you want to go to the top of the hill, turn to page 92.

You're not ready to tell anyone about the bottle. Keeping it hidden under your clothing, you start walking back to camp. You'll decide what to do tomorrow.

Suddenly, unseen hands grab you from behind. That is your last memory of ancient Egypt.

The next thing you see is the high ceiling of the Cragmore Planetarium. The speaker is still talking about the night sky in August. Did you fall asleep? Nothing seems to have changed, until you check your pocket. The old bottle is gone.

If you hurry, you may still have time to finish your term paper.

THE END

from page 16

All you can think to say is, "You're welcome."

"But now what is to become of me?" asks the ape. "Where will I go to live? No museum wants a live gorilla."

Just then Professor Brown shows up. He is glad to see you unharmed, but he is quite surprised to see a live gorilla.

"Don't worry, professor," you say. You tell him exactly what happened.

"Can *you* help me?" the gorilla asks Professor Brown. "I used to live in Africa."

"You could always live in the Metropolitan Zoo," you suggest. You want to help the gorilla find a good home, but you are afraid a museum watchman is going to stroll by any second.

Then Professor Brown says, "You know, I'm about to leave for a new digging expedition in Africa. You could come along with me on the ship. We could disguise you in some of my old clothing."

"I don't know," says the gorilla. He looks at you and asks, "What do you think?"

If you want to help the professor take the gorilla to the pier, turn to page 49.

If you want to take the gorilla to the zoo by subway, turn to page 55.

70

from page 21

You slip inside Dr. Walker's office and lock the door behind you. The floor is cluttered. Every shelf and desk is piled high with scientific journals, dinosaur fossils, and machine parts. Giant ferns unlike any you have ever seen grow under purple lights.

Suddenly a strange machine with two lights and two seats materializes in front of you. On one seat is an open notebook. The last date in it reads 33,005 B.C. Could this be a time machine?

That is all you have time to read. You hear a pounding on the locked office door. You look around and see that this office also has a back door. The time machine looks simple to operate.

If you want to try to escape by traveling through time, turn to page 86.

If you want to try to escape through the back door, turn to page 84.

from page 85

You do not want to touch another drop from this bottle. First it brought you to ancient Egypt. Is it now turning you into a bird?

Trying not to panic, you sit calmly in your hidden spot. In half an hour, the talons begin to fade and your feet return to normal.

Now you are not sure what to think. The liquid seems to do whatever it wants. From your secret spot, you have a good view of the pyramid workers' camp.

If you want to wait here and watch to see if Calik will leave camp again tonight, turn to page 63.

If you want to walk back to camp and keep the bottle a secret, turn to page 67.

from page 92

You walk out into the clearing. "I am a friend," you say.

They freeze you solid. When you thaw out, you will end up in a zoo somewhere in the Rigel star system.

THE END

from page 81

Standing in line will take too long. Perhaps this man is the only way to get a message to the pharaoh. But you can't say anything about the potion.

You tell the man that you want to meet the pharaoh in a grove of trees by the river. You tell him it is urgent.

As you wait by the river, you wonder when the pharaoh will arrive. He never does, but the Priests of Amun-Ra do.

THE END

74

from page 21

The Hall of Dinosaurs is a big room, but for some reason all the exits are blocked. The seven people now have you trapped. Giant dinosaur skeletons loom above you.

"Give us that bottle," says the leader.

If you want to give them the bottle, turn to page 83.

If you want to drink the potion, turn to page 89.

from page 92

You decide to remain hidden, to wait for a better opportunity to rescue Dr. Walker. Suddenly there is trouble with the ray gun. The aliens take the gun apart.

"Ekon!" you hear one grumble. "Borg" says the other. They can't seem to fix it.

Now you run into the clearing. The two aliens are so surprised, they run into their spaceship. But they leave the door open.

If you want to follow the aliens into their ship, turn to page 91.

If you want to try to take away the frozen Dr. Walker, turn to page 95.

from page 81

You decide to wait your turn in line. You wait ten minutes, then fifteen. The line is getting shorter. But the delay is too long.

Agents of the Priests have you arrested. The potion is taken from you, and the terror begins.

THE END

78

You tell Calik the whole story about how you found the bottle, then traveled back in time. Calik does not understand everything you are saying, but he feels you must be telling him the truth, especially when you show him the bottle.

"Thank you for telling me," says Calik. "That took great courage. Now there is not a moment to lose. The Priests are getting ready to attack, and we must get this bottle to the pharaoh in time. I am afraid I must ask you to take this to him yourself. I have other important business I must see to first.

"Beware of the Priests and their agents! Give this potion to no one but the pharaoh. Don't even speak of it to anyone else or we are all doomed. May the great god Ra be with you." Calik disappears down a dark street.

You begin walking to the pharaoh's palace.

Turn to page 81.

from page 18

Something inside you says these people should not get their hands on the bottle. "Don't come any closer," you say. "This bottle is the property of Cragmore Museum."

"There is no need to be emotional, young friend," says their leader in a soothing voice. "The bottle is only of historical curiosity and has no real value. But we will be happy to pay you a generous reward for it, as a way to thank you for finding it. We will give you $5,000 in American cash, on the spot."

If you want to accept their offer, turn to page 12.

If you want to refuse, turn to page 16.

from page 78

You arrive at the palace just after dawn. When you get to the front of the building, there are dozens of people trying to get in to see the pharaoh. They form a line outside the palace doors.

You tell a guard that you absolutely must get in first. But he just frowns and tells you to go to the end of the line. You see a servant with a breakfast tray going around a corner to the back of the palace.

A man with a beard comes up to you and says, "It may take all day to get in to see the pharaoh today. You may never get in at all."

Then he whispers, "I have a connection inside the palace. If you give me that ring on your finger, I will see to it that your message gets to the pharaoh immediately."

If you want to follow the servant with the tray, turn to page 61.

If you want to give this man your ring, turn to page 73.

If you want to wait your turn in line, turn to page 77.

from page 47

You decide to go higher into the hills, since that is the area the rebels know best. You scramble to higher ground and put up a brave fight, but your defense in the hills is just what the Voxons expected.

In the end, the Voxons win. You are brought with the rest of the surviving rebels to work in the Mines of Pluto.

THE END

from page 74

You give them the potion. That is all they want from you. They leave the room, and you are left alone. There is still time to finish your research, but you are in no mood for studying. You wonder who those people were and why they wanted that bottle so much.

THE END

from page 70

You run through the back door, but this time the seven people aren't fooled by the same trick. Three of them are waiting for you.

THE END

You sneak away to a hidden spot where you can be alone. Opening the bottle, you recognize the familiar scent of honey and cinnamon.

After you take a little sip, you feel a warmth in your stomach. But when you look down, you see your feet have turned into the talons of a bird.

If you want to drink more of the liquid, turn to page 58.

If you don't want to drink more, turn to page 71.

from page 70

You hop into the machine and check the dial to make sure it is set for 33,005 B.C., the last date in Dr. Walker's journal. You switch on the machine, and it begins to hum.

The office door breaks down and the people in robes move slower and slower toward you. They seem to be walking through a thick cloud of tiny lights, all the colors of the rainbow. Then you smell, hear, and see nothing.

The next thing you know, you are in a flat, grassy land. It is cold. Ahead of you looms a forest. Behind you a glacier spreads out over hundreds of square miles. Woolly mammoths are grazing not far away, but they don't seem to notice you. A few other animals stand peacefully nearby. You are finally safe from the seven people, and the bottle is still in your pocket.

But are you alone in this ancient world?

Turn to page 54.

from page 47

You decide to go to the forest. This is an excellent idea. The forest is new territory for the rebels, but also for the Voxons. Lord Snag expected you to fight in the hills.

You also have a secret weapon in the forest that no one is counting on: the forest people. They hate the Voxons for cutting down so many trees and for hunting their people for sport. The forest people rise up to help you, and the Andromedan rebels beat the Voxons badly.

Now it is just a matter of time before you drive Lord Snag from Andromeda forever. You are a hero.

THE END

You drink the entire contents in one gulp, and the clay bottle crashes to your feet. The seven people gasp. You feel cold, then warm. You see the dinosaur skeletons split into crystals of colored light.

The next thing you know, you wake up in a hot world. Large insects buzz overhead. You see a huge dinosaur—a triceratops—walking nearby. Another dinosaur plods along in a marsh. You must have just traveled back in time millions of years! The potion is gone. You have no way to return home.

Suddenly a red light streaks overhead and crashes a mile away. You run there as fast as you can.

You can't believe what you find: an alien spaceship. But you are not the first one to find it. The crash has attracted several hungry dinosaurs. Two helpless aliens have managed to escape from their craft. They are in danger of being eaten. And so are you.

If you want to try to save the aliens, turn to page 94.

If you want to run to safety, turn to page 97.

from page 38

"We have never met a meddler like you," their leader says to you. "Now we will make sure you never get in our way again."

Just then the freed mummy shakes his fists. He knocks out one priest, then another. You and the professors tie them up. Now you can call the police.

"I am grateful to you three brave warriors for your heroism," says the mummy in ancient Egyptian. "I only wish that I could now go back to the land of my ancestors. Is there any way that you can help me? I am already in your debt."

Dr. Brown translates for you, then replies in the same language, "Yes. I think we can help you. Tonight Dr. Karp and I are leaving on a tramp steamer. We are going on a new dig in North Africa. We can take you along."

You help the mummy back into his case. Then you all drive down to the pier in Dr. Brown's station wagon. Before the mummy case is loaded on the boat, the ancient pharaoh thanks you.

"May the gentle winds of Thebes always blow against your back," he says. Then Dr. Brown closes the case. The longshoremen think it is just another artifact.

You take a taxi home, full of ideas for your report on ancient Egypt.

THE END

P.S. You get an A.

from page 76

You run into the alien spaceship. Perhaps you can make the aliens free Dr. Walker. But as you enter, the door shuts. That is the last you see of the planet Earth.

THE END

92

from page 66

Your first task is to find Dr. Walker. Whatever is shiny on top of the hill may be a clue, so you walk up there as carefully as you can.

At the crest of the hill, you see something amazing: a large spaceship with its hatch open. Small silvery aliens are walking about, working with a ray gun. Beside the aliens stands a woolly mammoth, frozen solid.

As a bird flies overhead, an alien shoots it with the ray gun, freezes it, and brings it down gently. Then you notice a frozen saber-toothed tiger, several birds— and a woman in a white coat. It can only be Dr. Margaret Walker!

If you want to approach the aliens, turn to page 72.

If you want to remain hidden, turn to page 76.

You throw stones and sticks to distract the dinosaurs from the aliens. Your plan works. The dinosaurs go away. After the animals have left, you approach the aliens.

"Thank you, Earthling," they say. "But we are dying anyway."

"No you're not," you say. You rush to get them water. Your quick thinking saves their lives.

Now they can begin to rebuild their spacecraft. "We are from the twenty-third century," they explain. To thank you, they bring you back to your own time, to your own home.

In their time travels, the aliens have been to ancient Rome, Greece, and Egypt. Tonight, in your room, they happily tell you everything they discovered about these civilizations. By morning you are ready to hand in a wonderful term paper. You can't wait till their next visit. They have promised to take you along on their next trip.

THE END

from page 76

You try lifting the frozen Dr. Walker. To your surprise, she is light as a mushroom. You quickly carry her away down the hill. The aliens do not follow you.

You bring Dr. Walker down to the cave of the prehistoric people you met earlier. They seem to know Dr. Walker. Soon she thaws out and feels much better. She calls the cave people by name and is delighted to meet you.

"Thank you for being so clever in finding me," she says. "I programmed my time machine to return to Cragmore Museum should anything have happened to me."

Now you tell her the bad news. "A mammoth broke the time machine."

With the prehistoric people, you all go have a look at it.

"Don't worry," says Dr. Walker. "We can fix this. But first, how about some dinner?"

You have to agree. You haven't felt this hungry in ages.

THE END

from page 61

Before the pharaoh has a chance to speak, you blurt out your story and present him with the potion.

"Thank you," says the pharaoh. "I don't know who you are, but I am in your debt. Now I have the power I need to defeat the evil Priests of Amun-Ra. How can I repay you?"

You tell him that you only want to get back to your own time. He sends you to his magicians, and they help you. You only ask for one more thing before you return. You ask the pharaoh for some general information about his country. After all, you still have to hand in a term paper when you get back.

The pharaoh smiles and gives you a personal tour of his city. Then he gives you a special present before you return home.

You get a good grade on your term paper. And your parents will always wonder where you got the small gold statue of an eagle.

THE END

from page 89

You run off to find safety. The dinosaurs do not follow you. After a day passes, you go back to the site of the crash. The aliens are gone.

Since you have no way to get back to your own time, you turn the broken spaceship into a safe, cozy home for yourself. You live a solitary, happy life in the world of the dinosaurs.

THE END

from page 66

You follow the prehistoric couple to their cave home. The rest of their family is there, and they welcome you. You eat hot food and sleep soundly beside them that night.

The next day you walk up to the hill to see the shiny object, but it is no longer there. Later you try to fix the damaged time machine, but you have no luck.

You never do find Dr. Walker, but you live a long, simple life with the prehistoric people.

THE END